First published in 1994 by Ultimate Editions

© 1994 Anness Publishing Limited
Boundary Row Studios
1 Boundary Row
London SE1 8HP

This edition distributed in Canada by
Book Express, an imprint of
Raincoast Book Distribution Limited
112 East 3rd Avenue, Vancouver
British Columbia, V5T 1C8

Distributed in Australia by Treasure Press

A CIP catalogue for this book is available from the British Library.

ISBN 1 86035 015 1

Editorial Director Joanna Lorenz
Editorial Consultant Jackie Fortey
Designer Sarah Hodder

Printed and bound in China

A Storyteller Book

Peter Pan

by J.M. Barrie

Adapted by Lesley Young
Illustrated by Jenny Press

INDEX

It was bed time in the nursery, but John, Wendy and Michael didn't feel at all tired. Their parents, Mr and Mrs Darling, were going out to dinner.

"Take care of the children, Nana," said Mrs Darling.

"Woof!" barked the large dog who lived in the nursery and looked after them. She had just filled the bath and tested the water with her paw.

"You go first, Michael, you're the youngest," said Wendy.

"I don't want a bath," said Michael, but Nana scooped him up and carried him off on her back, howling.

When Mrs Darling came back into the nursery to say goodnight, she heard a strange noise at the window. She rushed over, just in time to see the shape of a small boy, trying to open it. But when she opened the window and looked outside, there was no one there.

"I think I know what he's looking for," she said. The day before, Nana had seen a boy at the window, and she had bounded over and shut it so fast that she had cut off his shadow. Mrs Darling had folded it and put it away.

Mr Darling was in a bad mood because Nana had rubbed against his black trousers, and left long dog hairs all over them. And now Michael was refusing to take his cough medicine.

"Why doesn't Daddy take some of the medicine to keep Michael company?" suggested Wendy. Two doses were poured out but, while Michael drank his, Mr Darling poured his into Nana's bowl. Nana plodded over and drank it, thinking it was a treat. What a face she made!

"Oh, poor Nana!" said all the children, and they made such a fuss of her that Mr Darling said crossly, "The proper place for dogs is outside." He took her out and chained her up in the yard.

Mrs Darling tucked the children up in bed and tiptoed out of the room. In the quiet, dark nursery the children yawned, stretched and soon fell sound asleep.

Suddenly a tiny ball of fire darted into the room, zig-zagged round it, and disappeared into a jug. There was a click at the window. It flew open and a boy stepped inside and walked round the room as if he was looking for something.

At last he said. "Tink, do you know where they've put it?" The ball of fire flew over and rested on a drawer of a chest, making a tinkling noise. The boy ran over, opened the drawer, and pulled out his shadow.

"Oh well done, Tinker Bell! What a clever fairy you are," he shouted. "But how am I going to stick it on again?"

He fetched a bar of soap that Nana had left behind, and rubbed it all over his feet. Then he soaped his shadow and tried to stick it on to his feet, but it wouldn't stick.

"I will never have a shadow again," wailed the boy, and he burst into tears.

He sobbed so loudly that Wendy woke up, sat up and said,
   "Why are you crying?"
   The boy jumped to his feet and asked. "Who are you?"
   "Wendy Darling. Who are you?"
   "Peter Pan," said the boy.
   "Where do you live?"
   "I live in Never-Never Land." He pointed to the dark
window. "It's second turning to the right, and straight on till
morning."

"What a funny address," said Wendy, "but you know you'll never stick your shadow on like that. I'll sew it on for you."

She jumped out of bed and fetched a needle and thread and Peter let her sew it on. It stung quite badly when the needle went in and out, but it was worth it. Soon he was dancing up and down the nursery, watching his shadow make patterns on the floor as he threw his arms and legs about.

"How old are you, Peter?" asked Wendy.

"I don't know," he said, "because I ran away from home when I was very, very young. I heard my parents talking about what I would do when I was grown up. And I don't ever want to be grown up," he added, stamping his foot and making his shadow jump.

Suddenly there was a tinkling noise from the chest drawer. Peter pulled it open and Tinker Bell flew out.

"Oh!" cried Wendy, "Is that a fairy?"

"Of course it's a fairy," said Peter matter-of-factly. "And don't say you don't believe in them, because every time some silly child says that, a fairy dies."

"Do you live alone, Peter?" asked Wendy, watching Tinker Bell flit round the room.

"No, I live with the Lost Boys. They all fell out of their prams when their mothers were looking the other way."

Wendy gasped and put her hands up to her mouth, but Peter went on, "It's not so bad – if they are not claimed within seven days, they are sent off to Never-Never Land. I am their Captain."

"It sounds like fun," said Wendy, "but what made you come to our nursery window?"

"I often come, to hear your mother telling you all bedtime stories. The Lost Boys have no mothers to tell them stories, so I go back and tell them yours. And I must go back now. They'll wonder where I am."

"Oh, please stay," begged Wendy.

"I've got a better idea," said Peter, "why don't you come with me? Then you can tell us all stories and tuck us in at night."

"But I can't fly," said Wendy.

"I can teach you."

"And John and Michael, too?"

"Of course."

John and Michael were shaken gently awake, and told about Never-Never Land. "There are Indians there," said Peter, "and mermaids in the lagoon and, of course, the pirates . . ."

"Did you say pirates?" asked Michael, rubbing his eyes.

"Yes," said Peter, "we're always having to fight them."

"Let's go," shouted John, punching his pillow.

They tried to fly around the nursery, flapping their arms behind Peter, but they couldn't get off the ground.

"Wait while I sprinkle some fairy dust on you," said Peter. "Now wiggle your shoulders like this." Suddenly they could all fly as easily as birds.

"Now, Tink, lead the way," said Peter, standing on the window sill. She shot ahead like a star, and Peter held Wendy's hand as they all floated out into the night sky.

A moment later, Mrs Darling, who had just come home, rushed into the nursery, with Nana at her heels. But they were too late. The beds were empty. The children were already on their way to Never-Never Land.

The Lost Boys were wondering where Peter was. Slightly Soiled, the eldest, was playing a tin whistle and dancing with an ostrich, while Tootles, Nibs, Curly and the Twins looked on. They wore fur skins, because it was winter, so they looked more like bears than boys.

"Sh! Listen!" whispered Nibs suddenly. It was their enemies, the pirates. The boys just had time to scuttle down the stairs they had made in hollow trees, to their home in a secret underground cave.

"Yo ho, yo ho!" sang Captain Hook, the pirate chief, as his men pulled him along on a sledge. He waved his right arm in time to the music. Instead of a hand, it ended in a shiny hook – which is where he got his name. Peter Pan had cut off his hand in a fight and thrown it to a crocodile. The crocodile liked the taste so much that, ever since, it had wandered over land and sea, licking its lips as it searched for the rest of Captain Hook.

Luckily for the pirate chief, the crocodile had swallowed an alarm clock, and he always knew when it was coming. Every tick-tock sent shivers from his head, with its long, greasy black curls, right down to his toes.

"I'll rest here!" shouted the Captain, hauling himself on to a huge mushroom. "I'm on fire!" he roared suddenly as he felt his seat getting hotter and hotter. When he leapt up, he found that he had been sitting on the chimney of the Lost Boys' home, which Peter Pan had disguised with the mushroom.

"Ha! Ha! I've got them, now!" cackled Hook. But then he thought he heard a ticking noise. He took to his heels and ran into the forest, with his fat first mate, Smee, puffing along behind him.

The Lost Boys clambered out of their tree trunks again.

"Look at that huge white bird," said Nibs, pointing at Wendy, flying overhead in her nightgown. Tinker Bell was jealous because Peter liked Wendy so much, and she shouted down to Tootles to shoot her. He aimed with his bow and arrow, shot up into the sky, and Wendy fell to the ground.

"It's not a bird – it's a girl!" cried the boys in horror, as Peter Pan flew down to join them.

"I'm all right," whispered Wendy. "The arrow hit a button."

"We won't move you," said Peter. "You rest there and we'll build your own Wendy house around you."

They made the house out of wood from the forest, and put John's top hat on the roof as a chimney. When it was finished, they all piled inside. There was even a fire in a grate, and the light flickered on a row of happy faces as Wendy told them the first bedtime story that was all their own.

When summer came, Peter took the children down to the lagoon, where the mermaids lived.

"There's one!" shouted John, pointing. She was sitting on a rock, combing her long hair. John managed to catch hold of her tail, but she wriggled away like an eel.

The children had all climbed on to the big rock, when they saw the pirate ship sailing towards them.

"Look!" said Peter. "They've got Tiger Lily – the chief of our friends, the Indians."

Over the years, Peter had learned to speak exactly like Captain Hook. "Let her go, lads!" he bellowed, in Hook's voice. So the pirates cut Tiger Lily loose. She jumped overboard and swam towards Peter.

"You fools," shouted Hook, "I'll capture her myself." He rowed over and jumped on to the rock.

"Quick! Row Tiger Lily to the shore," said Peter and sprang at the pirate chief. The boys took her off in Hook's rowing boat while Wendy watched Peter and Hook fighting fiercely on the slippery rock. At last Hook was exhausted, and had to swim back to the pirate ship.

Wendy was stranded on the rock, too tired to swim to shore, and the tide was rising fast. Suddenly a large kite came flying over the lagoon. Peter was able to reach up and catch its tail, and tie it round Wendy.

"Good luck," he shouted as she soared off towards land.

The water was already lapping Peter's feet, when a sea bird came floating past on its nest, which had been blown off the cliff by the winds.

"Just in time," cried Peter, as he shooed the bird off and leapt in. He held out his jacket to catch the wind, and sailed to shore.

One night, Wendy told the boys a story about a mother and father whose children flew away to Never-Never Land. "But they always kept the nursery window open, in case they came flying back one night," she finished.

"It's not like that," said Peter, sadly. "I went back to my nursery window, but the window was barred and there was another little boy sleeping in my bed."

"What if there are other children in our beds?" said Wendy in horror. "We'd better go home at once."

"Don't go," begged the Lost Boys.

"You can all come, too" said Wendy. "I'm sure Mother would love to keep you all." They were very excited then, and rushed off to pack their baby clothes.

"I shan't come," said Peter, "because then I would have to grow up."

"Well, always remember to take your medicine, when we're gone . . ." began Wendy, when suddenly they all heard loud clashings overhead.

"The pirates and the Indians are fighting," said Nibs.

At last the noise stopped. The Indians had been beaten, and had run off.

Hook bent down and listened at the mushroom chimney.

"If the Indians have won," he heard Peter say, "they'll beat the tom-tom."

"Aha!" said Hook, and he picked up a tom-tom the Indians had dropped and began to beat it.

"You're safe now," said Peter, not realising that they were being tricked. "Tink will show you the way."

So one by one, the children crept up the tree trunk stairs. Then the pirates pounced and carried them off to the pirate ship.

Hook himself lay in wait for Peter, but he never appeared.

"Well, he shan't escape," said Hook. "I heard the little mother tell him to take his medicine? A good idea!" He stretched his long arm down the chimney, poured poison into Peter's glass, and stole away.

Peter was feeling very lonely and sad, when Tinker Bell flew into the cave. "The pirates have got them!" she said.

Peter leapt up and grabbed his sword, and, as he stopped to take his medicine before he left, brave Tinker Bell flew into his glass and drank it. "It's poisoned," she said, in a weak voice. Her light began to grow very faint.

Peter stood in the middle of the cave and shouted, "Would all the children who believe in fairies clap their hands!" A thunderous noise of clapping echoed round the cave, Tinker Bell's light grew strong again, and she set off with Peter to rescue Wendy and the boys.

On the pirate ship, Hook lounged in a deckchair and bellowed, "Bring up the prisoners!" The boys appeared, followed by Wendy in a long cloak.

"Tie her to the mast," shouted the pirate chief, pointing his hook at Wendy.

"Now, which of you boys wants to be first to walk the plank? Don't be shy!" said Hook with a crooked smile. Just at that moment, there was a loud tick-tock.

"Quick!" screamed Hook, "Hide me! It's the crocodile!"

The sailors clustered round him, with their backs to the deck, so none of them saw Peter Pan climbing over the ship's side. In his hand was a ticking alarm clock. Peter tiptoed into the cabin.

When the ticking stopped, Hook said, "Right. Shall we start with you?" and prodded John with his hook.

At that moment that was a loud, wailing noise from the cabin.

"We're h-haunted," stammered Hook, beginning to tremble. "Send the children in," he said.

The children were pushed into the cabin beside Peter, and the noises grew louder until the pirates crowded together and shook with fear and screwed up their eyes. None of them saw the children creep out and hide on deck.

Peter untied Wendy and secretly took her place, hidden beneath her cloak.

"Get rid of the girl," shouted a pirate. "Everyone knows that girls bring bad luck on a ship."

"No one can save you, now," said Hook, shaking his hook at the figure in the cloak. Peter Pan threw back the hood and cried, "Wrong again, Hook!"

The pirates gasped as the children rushed out from their hiding places, armed with weapons from the cabin.

"They must be ghosts," shouted fat Smee. "Whatever was making that awful noise has killed them." The pirates threw themselves overboard in terror, and Peter Pan and Hook were left facing each other on the deck.

"This time, we fight to the finish," said Peter, waving his sword above his head.

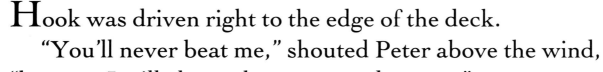

Hook was driven right to the edge of the deck.

"You'll never beat me," shouted Peter above the wind, "because I will always be young and strong."

He knocked Hook's sword away and pushed him over the side. Down below, the crocodile was waiting. It opened its mouth as if it was giving a huge yawn, and Hook fell right into its smiling jaws.

Back at home, the children's father and mother were sad and lonely.

"If I hadn't taken Nana out of the nursery, this would never have happened," said Mr Darling.

To punish himself, he decided to live in the dog's kennel until the children came home. He was carried to work in it and, when he came home, it was taken up to the nursery where Mrs Darling spent most of her time.

One evening, as Mrs Darling was sitting beside the fire in the nursery, she fell asleep. While she slept, three small figures flew in through the window and landed with soft thuds in their beds.

"Mother," called Wendy.

Mrs Darling woke with a start. So often she had dreamed that the children had come home. But this time, when she looked over, there were bumps under the quilts. Then the children threw back the covers and ran over to her.

"You've come home. At last!" she shouted, trying to put her arms round them all at once.

Mr Darling heard the noise and came rushing in, with Nana bounding behind him, barking joyfully.

When they had all calmed down a little, Wendy told her parents about Peter Pan and the Lost Boys, who were all waiting outside the window.

"You mean those poor children have no mothers?" said Mrs Darling. "Well, of course, they must come and live with us."

They all came in and sat beside the fire, as if they were waiting for a story.

"Will you stay, too, Peter?"

"I can't," he said, moving towards the window, "It would mean growing up. But I will miss you all."

"Why don't I fly to Never-Never Land every year, in the spring," said Wendy, "to make sure you're all right?"

"Then I'll keep the little house we made for you," laughed Peter happily.

"I'll put it up in the trees."

"But will you remember the way, Wendy?"

"Of course."

Peter Pan jumped on to the window sill, ready to fly, as Wendy and all the boys chanted together, "Second turning to the right, and straight on till morning."

So Peter Pan flew back to Never Never Land, the land where children never grow up; and as far as we know, he is there still.